For Matthew

To Heather—the girl with green eyes—and our wonderful sons,
Harry and George, who reminded me to look up at the stars—H. S.
To Bill Williams—P. C.
To my Mom and Dad—C. B.

Copyright © 2006 by Laika Entertainment

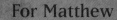

Story by Henry Selick; illustrations by Peter Chan; colored by Courtney Booker
Grateful thanks to Mike Berger for the original idea, and to Fiona Kenshole

First edition 2006

Library of Congress Cataloging-in-Publication Data is available.

Library of Congress Catalog Card Number 2006041647

ISBN-13: 978-0-7636-3068-3
ISBN-10: 0-7636-3068-3

2 4 6 8 10 9 7 5 3 1

Printed in China

This book was typeset in Matrix.
The illustrations were done in pencil and digitally colorized.

Candlewick Press
2067 Massachusetts Avenue
Cambridge, Massachusetts 02140

visit us at www.candlewick.com

MOONGIRL

Henry Selick

illustrated by Peter Chan
colored by Courtney Booker

CANDLEWICK PRESS
CAMBRIDGE, MASSACHUSETTS

Leon loved fishing in the moonlight. With Earl, his pet squirrel, perched on his shoulder, Leon tied a lightning bug to his hook as they drifted out on the bayou. He cast his line—reel singing, bait and bobber whistling through the air, then splashing down—when suddenly . . .

the moon went dark.

"Whatcha doing, Moonie?"
Leon grumbled. "I can't catch
supper with the lights out!"
Squinting in the dim light,
he took aim and cast once
more—but this time the rod
was yanked straight up, the
reel-drag ratcheting.

He'd caught something.
Something in the *sky*. It was
an enormous fish-of-stars.

"Holy moley!" cried Leon.
The giant fish took off, racing
across the sky, the tiny dinghy
dragged in its wake. Faster and
faster they went until the boat
was pulled right out of the
water and up, up, up into the
night sky.

"Yahoo!"

Leon howled with joy as the dinghy rocketed upward,
zigging and zagging behind the huge sparkling fish.

The big fish slowed, then smacked the boat with its giant tail, sending Leon and Earl head over heels into space. They were heading toward the moon!

"NOOOOooo!" cried Leon, shielding little Earl.

But instead of splatting into the crater-pocked surface, they crashed right through it as if it were paper.

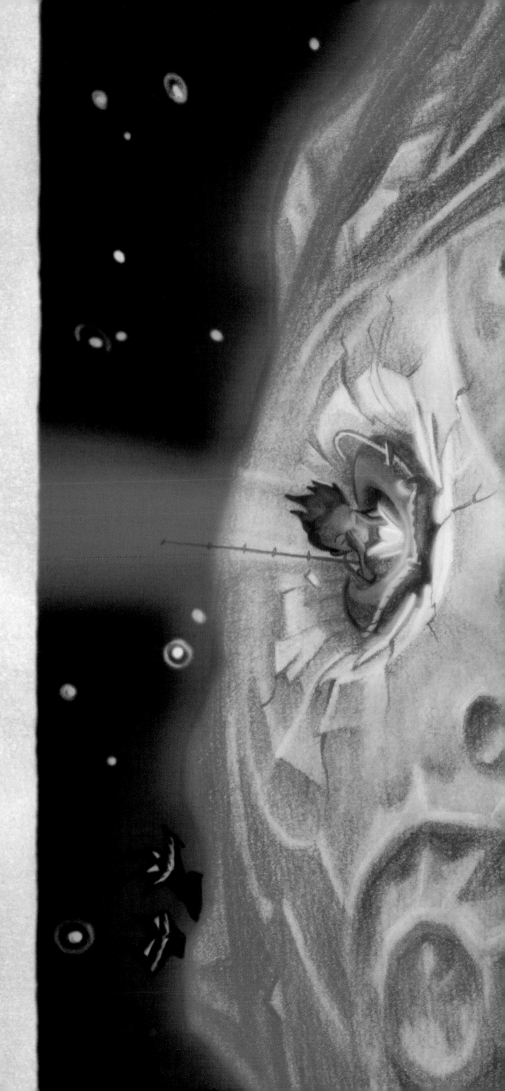

The dinghy bounced along and came to a stop in a glassy blue room. Huffing to catch his breath, Leon checked that Earl was safe in his pocket, then gazed slowly around. From the light of his glowing bait jar he could just make out the shape of an amazing carousel.

A voice startled him:
"Oh, good! Just what we need:
fresh lightning bugs."

Leon stared at the speaker.
It was a girl, strange and pretty,
with pale skin and large eyes.
Standing beside her was the
biggest cat he had ever seen.
Earl ducked into Leon's pocket
as the girl took the bait jar.

"Thanks, Leon," she said.
"Now, let's get cracking.
We've got to fix that crater you
made." She took his hand and
pulled him along. "I'm Moongirl."

Moongirl, thought Leon, smiling
to himself. He followed.

"What's your big cat doing?"
asked Leon as the creature poked
its head out through the hole Leon
had made.

"Siegfried is watching for the
gargaloon," Moongirl said.

"Garga-what?" asked Leon.
Earl popped up with a loud chirp.

Ears pricked, Siegfried pulled
his head back inside the hole
and spotted the little squirrel.
He licked his lips.

"The gargaloon is the monster
that lives on the dark side. It hates
moonlight. It will do anything to
keep the moon dark forever."

"Is it good to eat?"

"Uh, no," Moongirl answered.
"But it might eat us."

With a yowl, the big cat suddenly lunged at the squirrel.

"No, Siegfried!" yelled Moongirl. "Bad cat!"

The scaffolding pitched and yawed, and supplies tumbled. The work candle fell. No one noticed as the snaky, sneaky gargaloon slipped inside through the crater hole, snatched the jar of lightning bugs, and melted into the shadows.

Leon and Moongirl finished fixing the crater hole. "So what's that carousel for?" he asked.

Moongirl led Leon back toward the beautifully carved structure and showed him a set of controls. "This chain releases the brakes, this lever controls the music, and this one makes the animals go up and down," she said.

Leon still didn't understand. Why was there a merry-go-round inside the moon?

CLANG!

A glass jar banged against the railing of a staircase that rose to the top of the room. Moongirl's eyes widened in horror. "It's the gargaloon!" she cried. "And it's taken the jar!"

Leon stared at Moongirl. "They're just lightning bugs," he said.

Moongirl grabbed him by the shoulders. "No, Leon. Without fresh lightning bugs, we can't relight the room. And without moonlight, there'll be no more romance—or dreams."

Leon didn't care much about dreams. And he didn't care at all about romance.

"And there'll be no more night fishing," Moongirl added. Leon cared a lot about that.

Leon grabbed his fishing rod. "Let's get it!" They grabbed onto Siegfried's tail as the huge cat bounded to the top of the moon and out the hatch—right behind the gargaloon.

Just outside the hatch, Siegfried
landed in a pool of glue and
was stuck fast. The gargaloon
had set a trap.

"Poor Siggy," cried Moongirl.
The gargaloon was getting away.
"We'll never catch it now."

But Leon had an idea. He tied a
loop at the end of his fishing line
and held it out to Earl. When the
squirrel's grip was secure, he gave
Leon the ready signal.

"Hold tight, partner!" Leon shouted, casting his line as hard
as he could and sending the little squirrel into the air.
The gargaloon sprang forward.

But Earl wasn't an ordinary squirrel; he was a *flying* squirrel.
Just in time, he spread his wing flaps and zoomed upward,
barely missing the gargaloon's jaws.

He knocked the bait jar right out of the gargaloon's claws. Leon reeled in the fishing line as fast as he could, while Earl log-rolled the jar toward him. But the enraged gargaloon came tearing after the squirrel, snapping closer and closer at his tiny heels.

With a great pull, Siegfried unstuck himself and,
as Earl rolled past on the jar, took a powerful swipe
at the gargaloon.

SMACK!

It flew up into the air. They all watched as the monster
faded back, back, then disappeared over the horizon to
the dark side. "Hooray!" they shouted.

Moongirl led Leon back inside, then up the ladder at the center of the carousel. She unlocked a small door at the top.

"Now open the jar," she said.

"Are you sure?" Leon asked. Moongirl nodded.

Slowly he twisted off the cap. They watched as the glowing bugs flew up into the air in a perfect circle and then into the opening. The door closed behind them.

Moongirl reached up on tiptoes and placed Leon's empty bait jar on a high shelf next to another one, this one with the name *Lorelei* written on it.

As he looked around, Leon saw that there were many circular shelves above, filled with hundreds of empty jars, each with a name on it.

"Mount up, everyone!" called
Moongirl. Leon, Siegfried, and
Earl hopped onto the carousel.
The music started up.

As the carousel started to turn,
Moongirl jumped on next to Leon.
She reached way out and snatched
the brass ring.

The center column opened like
the petals of a flower, bathing
everything in radiant amber light.
They went up and down, up and
down. The glow of the lightning
bugs grew stronger and stronger
until the whole moon lit up like
a glorious round paper lantern.

When the ride ended, they climbed back out to the moon's surface. "That was a heck of a good ride!" Leon said.

"Glad you liked it," Moongirl said, handing him the key to the carousel. "Now it's your turn— Moonboy."

Leon wasn't at all sure. But Earl, chittering reassuringly, gestured around at the bright moonlight. Gradually, as Leon turned the word over in his mind, a smile came over his face.

"Moonboy . . ." he repeated.

The girl climbed onto Siegfried's back.
"Goodbye," she said. The big cat launched itself
into the night sky where the blue earth rose in
the distance.

"Goodbye," Leon said, waving. "Goodbye . . . Lorelei."

Earl and Moonboy watched as the cat and the girl
leaped from star to star toward home.